W9-BKB-677

BARBIE LOVES CHEERLEADING

By Rebecca Frazer • Illustrated by Karen Wolcott

Cover photography by Joe Dias, Susan Kurtz, Greg Roccia, Gerard Vuilleumier, and Judy Tsuno

A Random House PICTUREBACK® Book
Random House 🏠 New York

BARBIE and associated trademarks and trade dress are owned by, and used under license from, Mattel, Inc.
© 2007 Mattel, Inc. All Rights Reserved.
Published in the United States by Random House Children's Books, a division of Random House, Inc.,
New York, and in Canada by Random House of Canada Limited, Toronto.
No part of this book may be reproduced or copied in any form without permission from the copyright owner.
PICTUREBACK, RANDOM HOUSE, and the Random House colophon are registered trademarks of Random House, Inc.
Library of Congress Control Number: 2006928359   ISBN: 978-0-375-87485-7
www.randomhouse.com/kids   MANUFACTURED IN CHINA   10 9 8 7 6 5 4 3 2 1

"I'm so excited to see the big championship game tonight!" exclaims Stacie.

"Me too!" Barbie replies as they head into the stadium. "Before it starts, let's visit the cheerleading squad. I want you to meet some of my friends."

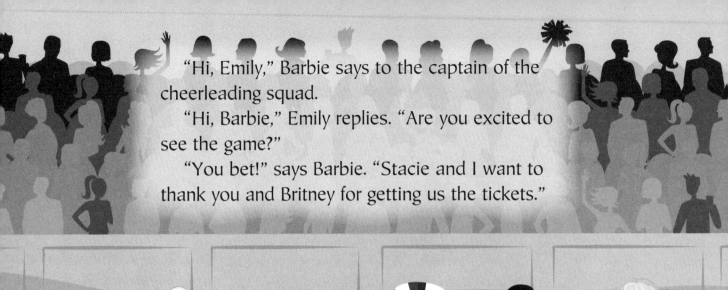

"Hi, Emily," Barbie says to the captain of the cheerleading squad.

"Hi, Barbie," Emily replies. "Are you excited to see the game?"

"You bet!" says Barbie. "Stacie and I want to thank you and Britney for getting us the tickets."

Ring! It's Emily's cell phone. Britney has sprained her ankle—and won't be able to cheer at the game!

"What are you going to do?" Barbie asks.

Emily has an idea. . . .

"Barbie, do you still remember the cheers we used to do when you were a cheerleader?" Emily asks. "Maybe you could fill in for Britney tonight. We have an extra uniform."

"I don't know," says Barbie. "I haven't cheered in a while. I'm totally out of practice."

"Go for it, Barbie!" cheers Stacie.

"Okay. I'll do it!" Barbie agrees.

"A perfect fit!" Emily says when Barbie tries on the cheerleading uniform.

"Thanks," replies Barbie. "But I'm a little nervous about all this."

"Don't worry," Emily says. "You'll be great. Let's go practice before the game starts!"

Barbie and the cheerleading team practice their jumps . . .

. . . cheers . . .

. . . and stunts.

"Way to go, Barbie!" Emily calls.

Suddenly, the whistle blows. The game is about to begin!
"Ready? Okay!" shouts Emily, starting the first cheer.
Barbie remembers all the steps and doesn't miss a beat! The
entire squad follows the captain with amazing dance moves.

It's a very exciting and very close game. Right before halftime, the visitors get a touchdown and take the lead! "We've got to get the crowd and our team charged up," Barbie says. "Let's do a really special cheer!"

The cheerleaders make a pyramid—and the crowd goes wild!

The home team is charged—and comes back after halftime to win the game! Everyone claps, cheers, and hollers for the champions.

"That was so cool!" exclaims Stacie after the game. "You're an awesome cheerleader, Barbie! And guess what? I've got a special cheer just for you.

With cartwheels, pom-poms, smiles, and pep,
Barbie doesn't miss a step!
She's really cool and so much fun.
She's my sister—she's number one!"

Barbie loves her sister's cheer and gives her a big hug. "Thanks for your great cheer," says Barbie. "Hooray for cheerleading!"

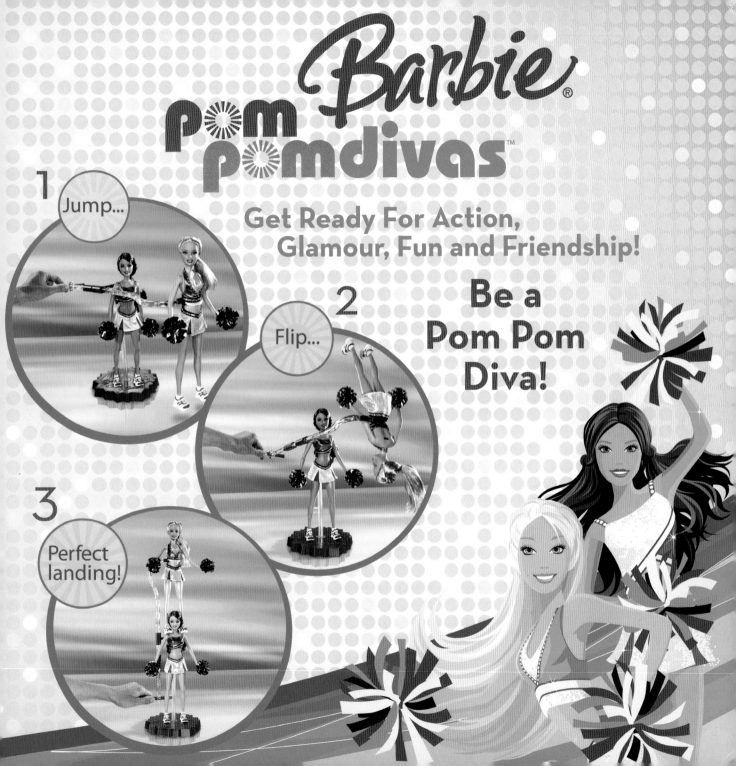

Barbie® pom pomdivas™

Get in on the action! Pom Pom Divas™ Barbie® and Teresa,® along with their Twirl Girl™ friends Summer® and Nikki,® are dressed to impress and can really flip and twirl! Practice makes perfect and it's time to compete!

Kick

Shake

Cart Wheel

Twirl Girls™ –
Summer® and Nikki® dolls

Fly Girls™ –
Barbie® & Teresa® dolls

Electronic Diary

Performance Playset™
(Doll is not included)